KEY LANDMARKS CIRCA 1930

I. John Muir Elementary School

II. Le Conte School

III. Merced Public Library

IV. Merced County Courthouse

V. Merced City Hall

VI. Tioga Hotel

VII. Merced Theatre

VIII. Montgomery Ward Department Store

IX. El Capitan Hotel

X. Bank of Italy (Mondo Building)

XI. Hartman's Department Store

XII. Ah Quong Laundry

This book belongs to:

For all whose stories shape our own.

With special thanks to my beloved Gerrit.

Library of Congress Cataloging-in-Publication Data

(CIP data on file)
ISBN 978-1-62972-779-0

Printed in China   6/2020
RR Donnelley, Dongguan, China

10 9 8 7 6 5 4 3 2 1

Ming's Christmas Wishes

Written by Susan L. Gong • Illustrated by Masahiro Tateishi

SHADOW
MOUNTAIN

"Not this year." Mrs. Chatlin waved Ming off.

"Not this year," Ming repeated, her voice rising. "Not last year. Not the year before that. Not next year. You will never let me sing in the Christmas choir because I'm . . ."

"Headstrong?" the teacher said, turning away.

"Chinese," Ming whispered. "I wish I could be part of the choir."

Ming caught sight of the clock. It was late. She knew she wouldn't have dinner ready on time. Mama would be angry.

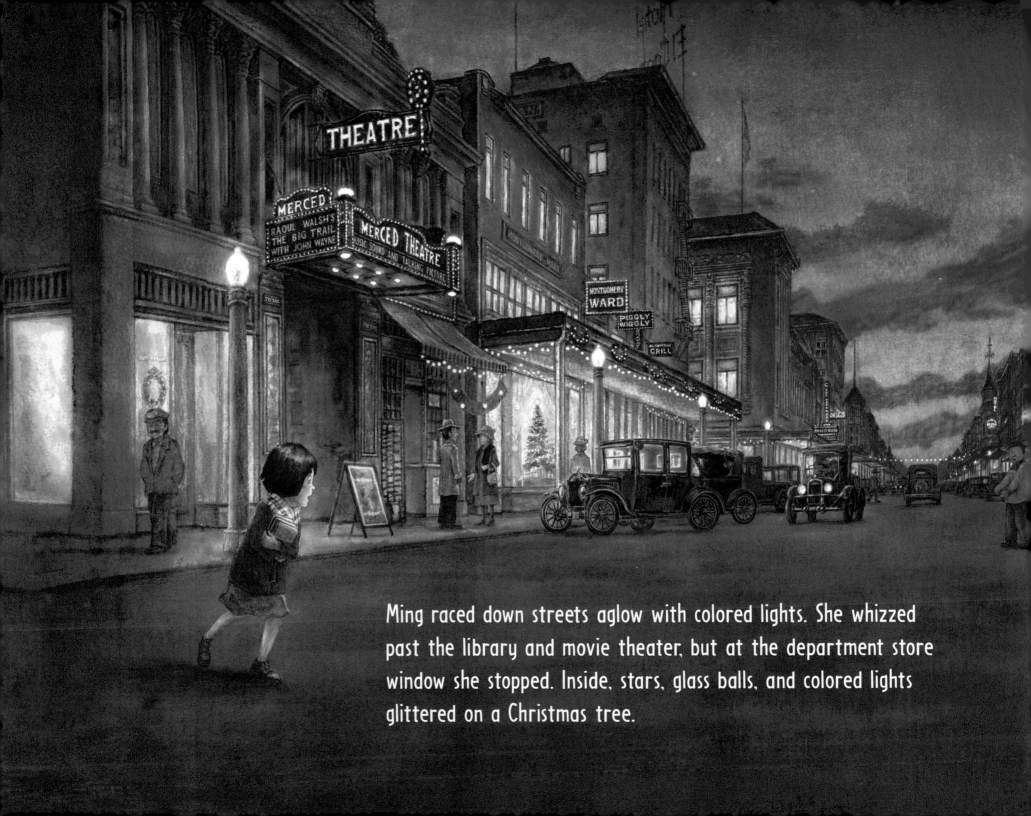

Ming raced down streets aglow with colored lights. She whizzed past the library and movie theater, but at the department store window she stopped. Inside, stars, glass balls, and colored lights glittered on a Christmas tree.

"*Wa!*" Ming whispered. "So beautiful! I wish my family could have a Christmas tree."

She stared at the dazzling tree. "Hmm," she thought, "anyone can have a Christmas tree. I just have to convince Mama!" She pushed herself away from the window and sped home.

Ming slipped into the warm kitchen. She pulled a bowl from the shelf and grabbed the flour scoop. She made Mama's favorite, noodles as fine as dragon whiskers.

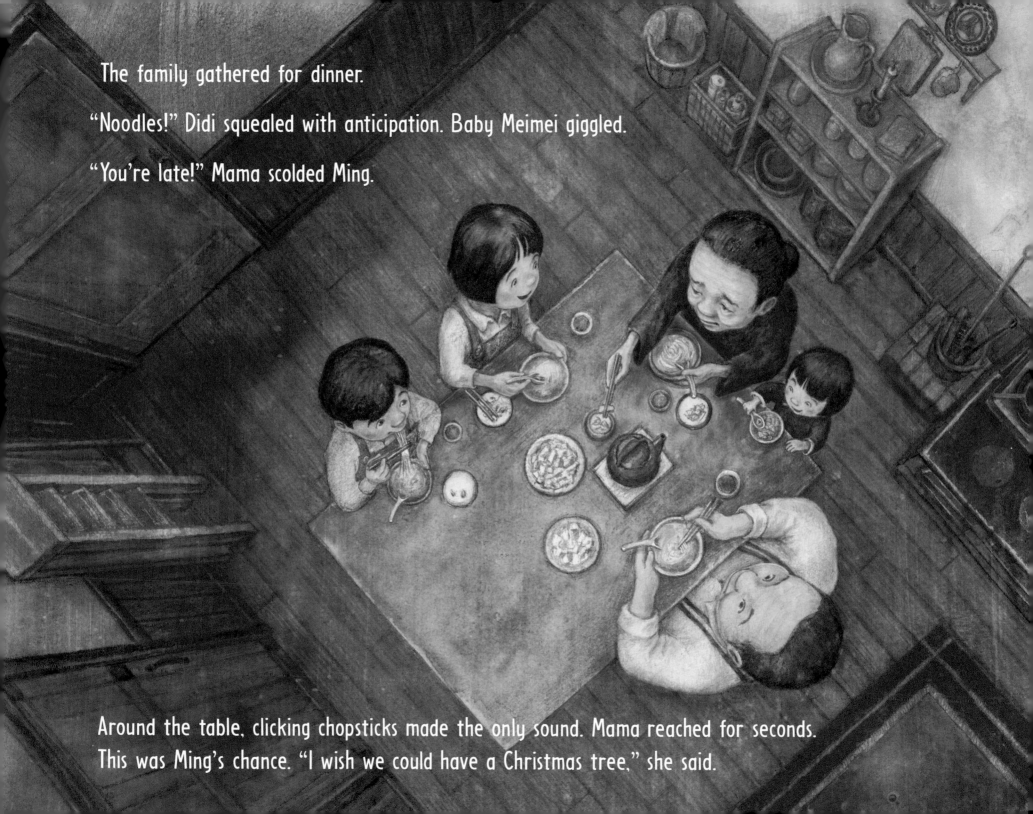

The family gathered for dinner.

"Noodles!" Didi squealed with anticipation. Baby Meimei giggled.

"You're late!" Mama scolded Ming.

Around the table, clicking chopsticks made the only sound. Mama reached for seconds. This was Ming's chance. "I wish we could have a Christmas tree," she said.

"Silly idea," Mama said.

Ming twirled noodles in her spoon. "It wouldn't have to be fancy."

"Could we have candy?" Didi asked. "Louie's family gets candy."

"No!" Mama said emphatically. "Christmas trees are not Chinese. No tree. No candy."

"But, Mama, we're in America," Ming insisted. "Every family here has a Christmas tree."

Mama glared at Ming. "NO CHRISTMAS TREE!"

Everyone froze.

Finally Pop said, "What Mama says goes." He patted her hand.

"Mama, I have to visit the Lins tomorrow. I'll take Ming with me so she won't be in your way."

Ming woke the next morning in velvety darkness. Outside, ground frost shimmered. Ten thousand stars in the Great Silver River glittered across a black sky.

She dressed, lit the stove, and lifted a pot to cook *juk*, rice porridge. She packed lunches in flat tin boxes.

A whole day with Pop! She hoped it would be enough time to help him understand why the family just had to have a Christmas tree.

Pop padded in. "Morning, Butterfly."

Ming placed the bowls of *juk* on the table.
She shoveled food into her mouth but Pop never hurried.

After what seemed a timeless-long time, he said, "Okay,
Butterfly. Let's go!"

Pop tossed a burlap bag in the back of their old truck. It landed with a clank.

Ming climbed on the running board and slipped into the cab. Pop squeezed behind the wheel and turned the key. The old truck chugged eastward. Dawn crept across the valley, waking the oak and sage of the chaparral. Clouds huddled against the mountains ahead.

As the truck rumbled into the foothills, Ming spied a pine tree. "Hey, Pop, look!"

"Hmm," he said. The road got steeper. The engine groaned. Pop patted the dashboard to coax the truck forward. They crossed stone bridges. Firs and pines pressed thick and tall against the road.

"That one's perfect!" Ming pointed to a symmetrical fir.

"Did I say we'd get a tree?" Pop asked.

It began to snow.

"Your grandfather called this his mountain," Pop said.

"Hmm," Ming said.

They rounded a corner. A village materialized in the snow.
Pop turned the truck off the road and parked it in front of a shack.

The stairs creaked under Ming's feet.
The door opened before Pop could knock.

A toothless man looking like an immortal carved from a crooked branch greeted them. Pop bowed respectfully.

The old man's eyes disappeared in a deep crease. "Old friend!"

"Uncle Lin!" Pop said. "You remember my daughter." He signaled Ming to bow.

Uncle nodded and then called behind him, "Father!"

An even more ancient man huddled under a quilt on a bed in the corner.

"Father!" Uncle Lin shouted again. "Old Gong's son is here."

"Your father was my best friend." Grandfather Lin's voice was as faint as an echo.

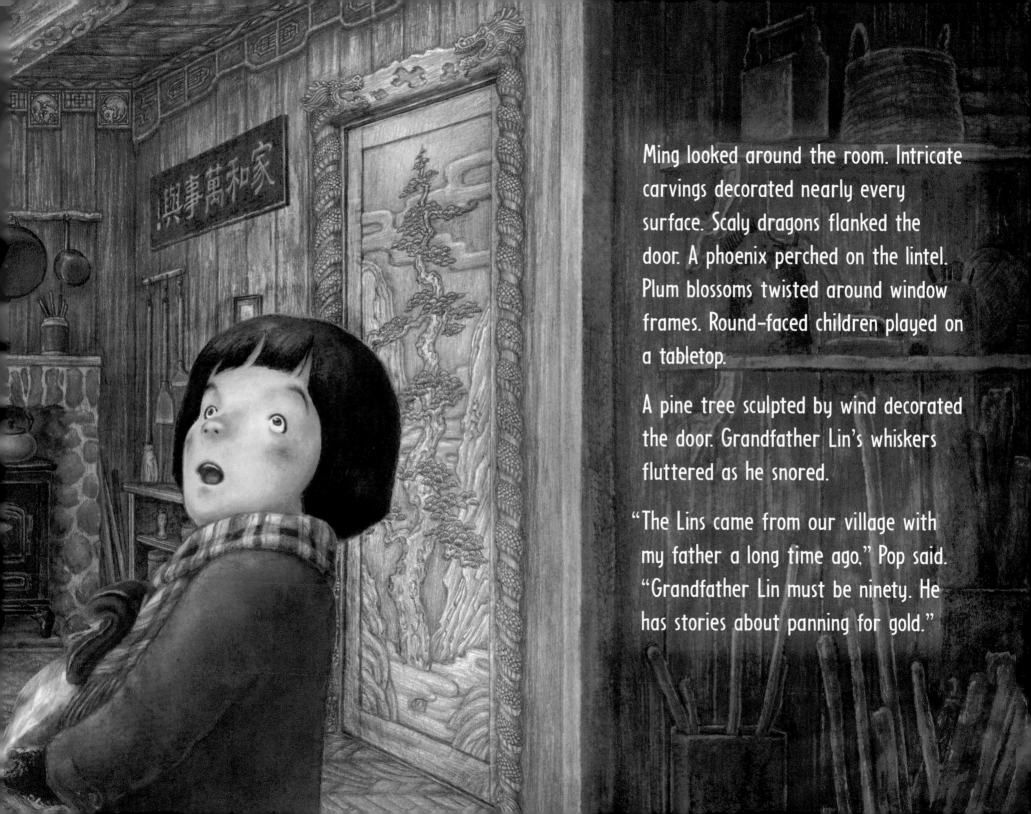

Ming looked around the room. Intricate carvings decorated nearly every surface. Scaly dragons flanked the door. A phoenix perched on the lintel. Plum blossoms twisted around window frames. Round-faced children played on a tabletop.

A pine tree sculpted by wind decorated the door. Grandfather Lin's whiskers fluttered as he snored.

"The Lins came from our village with my father a long time ago," Pop said. "Grandfather Lin must be ninety. He has stories about panning for gold."

Uncle Lin served tea and watermelon seeds. They shared the lunch Ming had made. Afterward, Ming sucked on the salty seeds while the men talked about adventures from their past. Eating dim sum in Hong Kong. Rambling through Yosemite. Hopping a summer train to Canada.

They remembered waking to the rumble of San Francisco's Great Quake and escaping the terrible fire by fleeing to a pier.

"We lost everything," Uncle Lin said.

"Yes, but we started again," Pop said.

They had cut their black braids to show support for revolution in China and had posed for photos to send their picture brides—the young women in China their families had arranged for them to marry.

"Your carvings grow more wonderful every year," Pop said. "That pine tree is especially beautiful."

"Pines for long life," Uncle said. "For strong character."

Pop gestured toward the older man. "If you two want to move to town, there is always a place for you with us."

"We're content," Uncle Lin said.

Pop thanked the Lins for generations of kindness.

Uncle smiled. "We are forever in debt to the Gongs." Their words were as comfortable as old silk.

"I'm taking Ming to the old grove," Pop said.

"Can you find it?" Uncle asked.

"With my eyes closed," Pop said.

Grandfather Lin whispered from the corner, "Safe journey!"

"May you live a hundred years," Pop returned.

White blanketed the world as Pop turned the truck from the main road onto a gravel path.

"Where are we going? Ming asked.

"Hmm," Pop said.

The truck chugged toward a grove of towering trees. Pop cut the engine.

The trees stood so tall their tops disappeared in swirls of snow, so enormous they breathed a hush that filled the forest, so strong they held up heaven. Ming ran her hand across their rough bark. She walked heel-to-toe around a tree.

"Ninety-two, ninety-three, ninety-four," she whispered. "*Wa!*"

"Sequoias," Pop said. "They've been here forever."

They walked deeper into the grove. Pop led Ming to a huge, lopsided tree. He pointed to a hollow at its base. "See?"

Ming spied a small wooden altar sheltered in the shadows. "Where did that come from?" she asked.

"Chinese miners left it here ages ago," Pop said. Kneeling, he took two incense sticks from his pocket. He lit one stick and placed it by the altar. Ming lit the second.

"I was fourteen when I came from China, Butterfly. I worked with my father in San Francisco. When there was trouble, he brought me to this mountain. 'Here,' he said, 'we are not foreigners. Here we are men, a small part of nature's greatness.'"

"Grandfather's mountain," Ming said.

Snow settled like a whisper on her shoulders.

"Pop," Ming asked, "when you light incense, what is in your heart?"

"A wish, a prayer that my children will make their way."

"Who hears your prayers, Pop?" asked Ming.

"Guanyin, the Goddess of Mercy, I hope. Or ancestors who will help my children."

Ming hesitated. "Pop," she said, "I don't fit in at school and I don't fit in at home. What's going to happen to me?"

He sighed, "You push too much, Butterfly. Pushing tips you off balance. Maybe you get hurt. Maybe you hurt somebody. Either way, pushing Mama won't make you happy." He looked deep into Ming's eyes. "She is a good woman."

"But she pushes me!" Ming said.

Pop sighed. "Hers is a hard story, Butterfly."

Incense burned low. Embers cooled.

They retraced their steps through the trees to the truck. Pop pulled the burlap bag from the truck bed.

"Do you know what that is?" Pop asked, pointing to a crooked tree at the edge of the grove.

"A sequoia?" Ming guessed.

"No," he laughed, "I'd never dig up a sequoia."

"Dig it up? But Mama said no Christmas tree."

"Ah, but this is not a Christmas tree," Pop said. "This is a Chinese pine—for long life."

"For strong character!" Ming said.

Pop pulled a small shovel from the bag. In his strong hands the tool did its job quickly. They loaded their prize onto the truck, slipped into the cab, and rumbled down Grandfather's mountain.

Ming closed her eyes, "I wish," she whispered, "this day could last forever."

聖 誕 節 快 樂

May you have a wonderful Christmas!

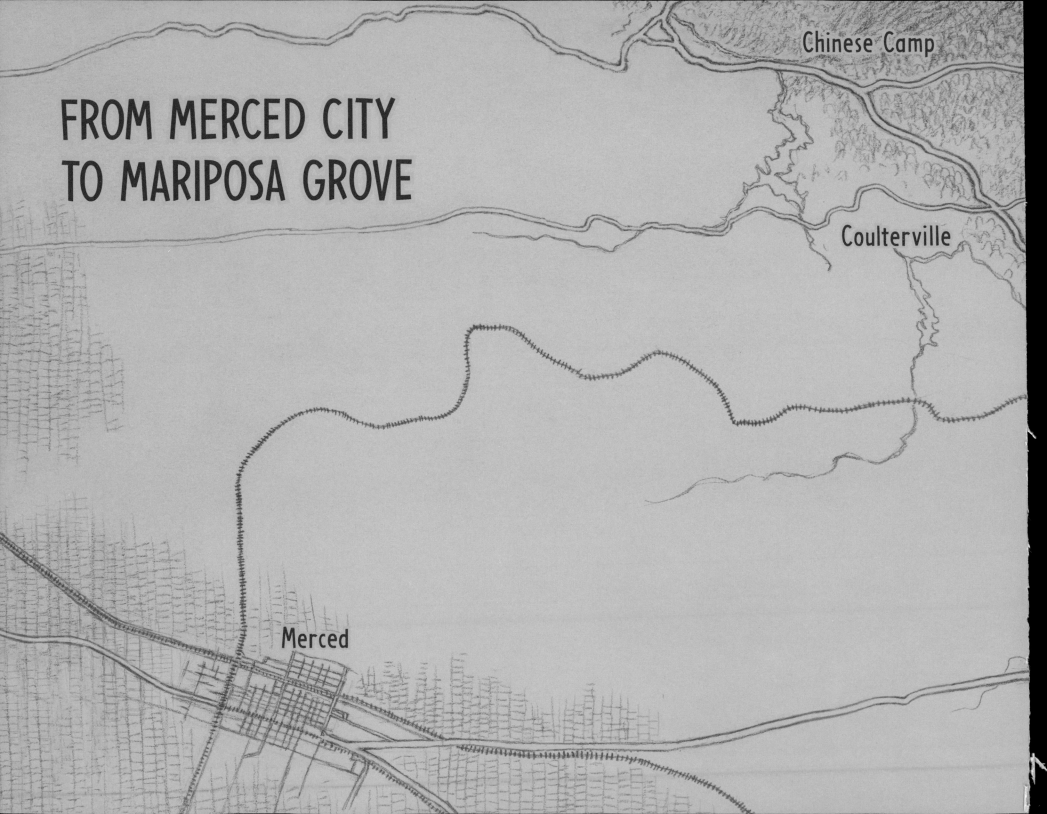

FROM MERCED CITY
TO MARIPOSA GROVE

Chinese Camp

Coulterville

Merced